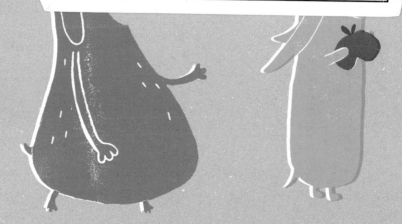

This book belongs to

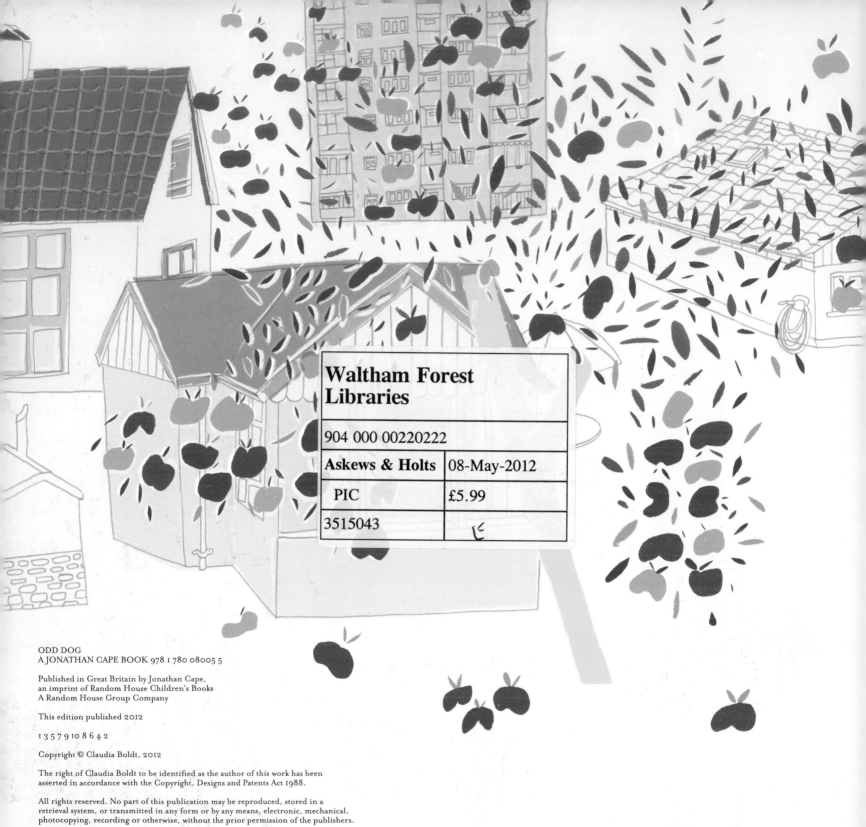

ODD DOG
A JONATHAN CAPE BOOK 978 1 780 08005 5

Published in Great Britain by Jonathan Cape,
an imprint of Random House Children's Books
A Random House Group Company

This edition published 2012

1 3 5 7 9 10 8 6 4 2

Copyright © Claudia Boldt, 2012

The right of Claudia Boldt to be identified as the author of this work has been
asserted in accordance with the Copyright, Designs and Patents Act 1988.

RANDOM HOUSE CHILDREN'S BOOKS
61–63 Uxbridge Road, London W5 5SA

www.kidsatrandomhouse.co.uk
www.randomhouse.co.uk

Addresses for companies within The Random House Group Limited can be found at: www.
randomhouse.co.uk/offices.htm

THE RANDOM HOUSE GROUP Limited Reg. No. 954009

A CIP catalogue record for this book is available from the British Library.

Printed and bound in China

For Gustav and Sebastian

CLAUDIA BOLDT

Odd Dog

Jonathan Cape · London

Helmut

Helmut was an odd dog.
Unlike all the other dogs he did not
care for bones, but he loved apples.
His apple tree was his pride and joy.

Helmut loved the apples from his tree so much that he was always worried his neighbour, Igor, was plotting to steal them.

At night, Helmut dreamed about
his apple tree.

Sometimes he would wake up so worried
that he couldn't get back to sleep.

And sometimes he would have
nightmares that Igor had found
a way to steal one of the apples
or – even worse – all of them.

So he counted them every morning, just to make sure.

One day, disaster struck!

The juiciest apple of all was just about to fall into Igor's garden.

There was no time to lose!

Helmut tried everything . . .

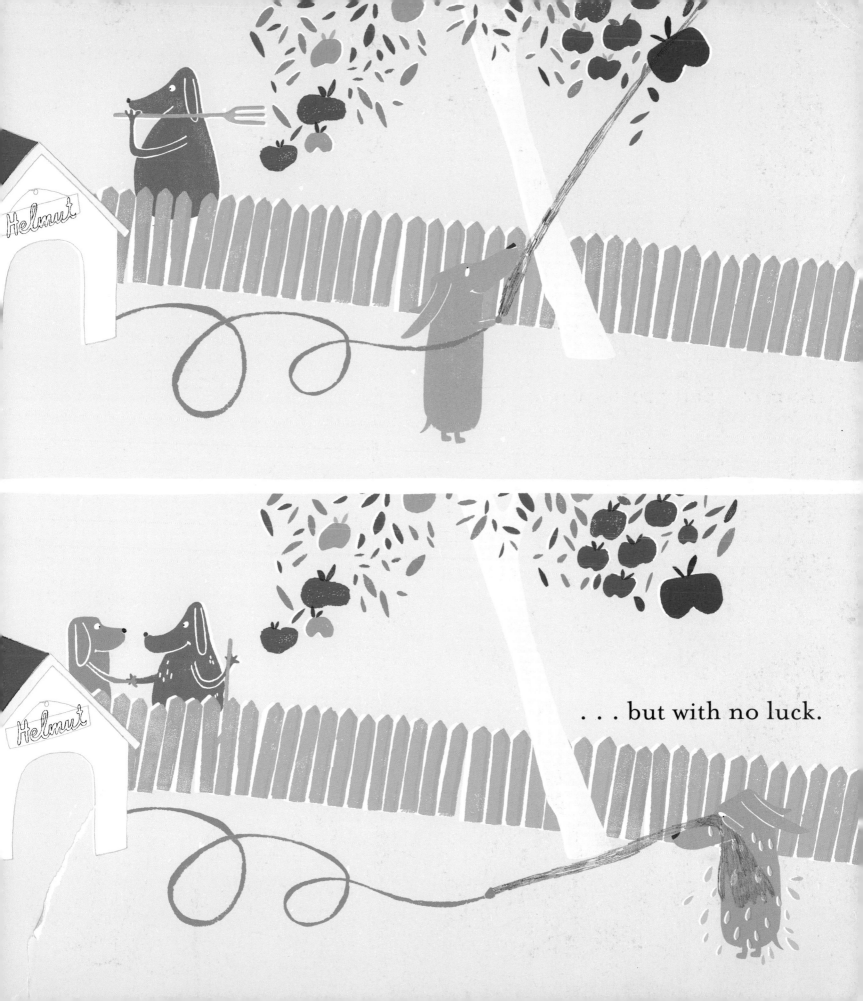

. . . but with no luck.

"Igor's going to get my best apple –
just like he always gets everything,"
Helmut thought. "It's not fair!"

Helmut was feeling
dreadfully sorry
for himself, when
all of a sudden . . .

nooooo!

. . . the apple fell.

Klong!

The apple landed in Igor's bowl.

But instead of eating the apple, Igor said,
"Here you go, Helmut! This apple looks
very ripe and juicy, and I know how much
you love them."

Helmut was very surprised. "Oh," he said.
"Thank you. Um . . . Would you like a bite?"

"No, thank you very much," said Igor.
"I don't really like apples. I love bones."

Helmut wanted to thank Igor for returning the apple, so he invited him for a picnic.

And from that day on . . .

. . . they were the very best of friends.